Jillian Jiggs

Written and Illustrated by Phoebe Gilman

SCHOLASTIC INC.

New York Toronto London Auckland Sydney

43108

JUN 1 8 1991

ISBN 0-590-41340-6

Copyright © 1985 by Phoebe Gilman.
All rights reserved. Published by Scholastic Inc.,
730 Broadway, New York, NY 10003, by arrangement with North Winds Press.

12 11 10 9 8 7   9/8 0 1 2 3/9
Printed in the U.S.A.   23
First Scholastic printing, February 1988

A long time ago, when she was quite small,
Jillian Jiggs wore nothing at all.

"Those were the days," her mother would sigh,
As she looked round the room and started to cry.
For Jillian Jiggs liked to dress up and play,
And this made a mess in her room every day.

"Jillian, Jillian, Jillian Jiggs!
It looks like your room has been lived in by pigs!"
"Later. I promise. As soon as I'm through,
I'll clean up my room. I promise. I do."

Now, Jillian meant every word that she said,
But later the promise flew out of her head.
When Rachel and Peter started to shout,
Jillian had to, just had to go out.

"Oh, look at the boxes! Yippee! Hooray!
It's hard to believe someone threw these away.
I'm mad about boxes. Boxes are fun.
No one will guess who we are when we're done."

No one would guess...

But a mother would know.
A mother could tell by the tip of a toe.

"Jillian, Jillian, Jillian Jiggs!
It looks like your room has been lived in by pigs."
"Later. I promise. As soon as I'm through,
I'll clean up my room. I promise. I do."

"We'll help, Mrs. Jiggs. We'll do it. Don't worry.
We'll all work together. We'll clean in a hurry."
They started to clean up her room, it is true.
They started to clean, but before they were through...

Jillian thought up a game that was new.
They had to stop cleaning. What else could they do?
"Let's dress up as pirates. Tie sails to the bed.
Heave ho, you landlubbers! Full speed ahead!"

They dressed up as dragons.

They dressed up as trees.

They dressed up as bad guys who never say please.

They dressed up as chickens, cooped up and caged.

They turned into monsters who hollered and raged.

They cackled like witches. They stirred and they boiled.

Then they were royalty, pampered and spoiled.

They tiptoed and twirled like little light fairies.

They made themselves wings and flew like canaries.

Whenever they thought that was it, they were through...

She'd change all their costumes and start something new.

Then Jillian's mother came in with her mop,
Took one look around and...

29

...fainted, KERPLOP!

"Jillian, Jillian, Jillian Jiggs!
It looks like your room has been lived in by pigs!"
"Later. I promise. As soon as I'm..."

"Start cleaning this minute, this second, not later!
I want this room tidy. I want this room straighter!"

"You'd better go now, Rachel and Peter.
See you tomorrow when everything's neater."